Strum and The Wild Turkeys

*Life's a journey, not a destination, but if you
find yourself gathered in a beautiful space
surrounded by people who build you up,
you have already arrived.*

The Glina Brothers

Written by Noa Daniel

Illustrated by Alana McCarthy

The animals gathered in their usual place to check in with each other after a long cold winter.

The raccoons stood on the stage commenting as each forest animal joined the clearing.

Rooster, standing like a guard at the gate, counted the mice, the deer, the rabbits, the fox families, the chipmunks, the mama bear and her two new cubs, and the rest of the creatures that were coming together to mark the first day of Spring.

There had been a family of peacocks that joined the event each year, but this year they were nowhere to be found.

Everyone looked forward to their yearly parade of plumes. Their majestic feathers were a colorful addition to the Spring celebrations. Even Strum's plume, though smaller and less colourful, was something to look forward to for everyone.

That was, everyone except Strum.

Strum worried about his feathers.
They were green, blue and bronze,
like his brother's, but they weren't
quite as full or as dazzling.

Even though his sisters' plumes were
less colorful, like all female peacocks
(or peahens, as they're called), they
fanned their feathers with such
fantastic style that even their
plain plumes still outshined Strum's.

His siblings wore their feathers with pride while Strum wore his across his body to hide his less-than-full fan.

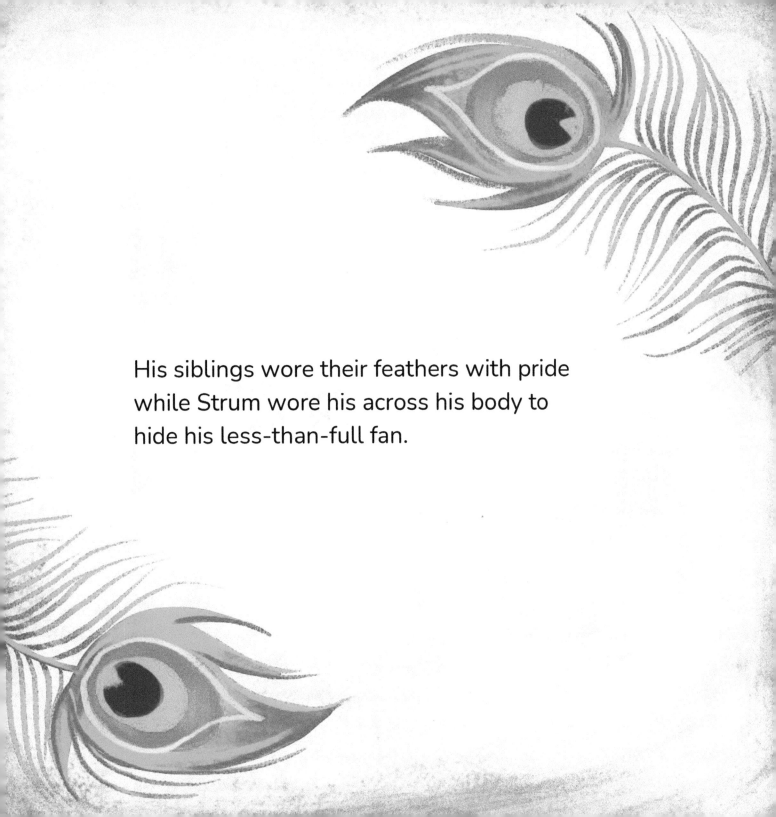

Strum felt different than his siblings. Every aspect of their lives left him feeling like he wasn't really a part of the party of peacocks that were his family. Strum's brother and sisters made their peacock sounds by shaking their feathers in perfect harmony.

Strum didn't like to shake the tail feathers that he tried to hide. Instead, he strummed them like a guitar, which is how he got his name.

His siblings laughed at how he played and made fun of every sound he made.

Strum called it *his* music and played to his own beat, in spite of their teasing.

His sister reminded Strum that, "A peacock's plume is a source of pride, with feathers flowing in patterned perfection." She added giggling, "A peacock without a beautiful plume is like a queen without a crown or a tiger without stripes."

Strum found comfort in picturing a beautiful stripeless white tiger and a queen on whom he had rarely seen a crown.

One day, the peacocks decided it was time to go find mates and get married. They set off on a long journey.

They didn't even ask Strum if he wanted to come.

Being alone can sometimes feel amazing, like everything is possible. Other times, it can feel really lonely.

Strum wasn't sure if he felt more alone *with* his brother and sisters or *without* them.

Strum sat on his perch playing his plume and singing his heart out to the moon.

Different is good...be yourself...
you don't have to look like, talk like,
walk like anybody else....

One morning, Strum noticed a flock of turkeys walking under his tree. He had been working on a new song when he looked down and saw them looking up from underneath him. He froze. Then, one of the turkeys said, "Don't stop."

Unsure, Strum just stared back.

"We've been listening to you play for a while, and we came to join you."

Cutt, Gobble, Kee Kee, and Yelp encouraged Strum to just play. The pitch of Strum's plume balanced Cutt's loud drum beats, Gobble's guttural gurglings, Kee Kee's keytar, and the tap of Yelp's tambourine. The five looked at each other.

Note after note, quietly at first and then louder, they were listening to each other and really blending their sounds. They were in sync.

Strum moved down his tree and joined the group.

They knew that they were on to something wonderful.

The sun set and rose overhead a few times, and the group played on. Strum felt a warmth inside of him that he had never known.

They quickly went from a bunch of musicians jamming together to something better.

Later that Spring day, as the gathering crowd grew
restless, the turkeys finally strolled down the path.
Their newest addition proudly led with his head high,
looking a little brighter and bolder than anyone had
seen before.

Strum took the stage, and
The Wild Turkeys began to play.

The band rocked the Spring gathering
...and many others to come.

Want to do more with this book?
Check out:
strumandthewildturkeys.com

Noa Daniel has been a classroom teacher for 25 years. She is also a speaker, podcaster, and consultant. Noa constructs projects and initiatives that amplify voice, build community, and propel engagement for learners of all ages. She is always *building outside the blocks.*

Noa lives just outside Toronto, Ontario, Canada with her husband and three daughters who all love music.

www.buildingoutsidetheblocks.com

Alana McCarthy is an illustrator, letterer, and designer who lives in Toronto with her husband, two boys and big orange cat Pumpkin. Her eye-catching imagery has graced kids books, magazines, product packaging, murals, ads and more. Over her award winning 20 year career she's worked with amazing clients such as *Disney/Pixar, Nickelodeon, Taco Bell, Cadbury, Coca Cola, Scholastic* and *Penguin Books.*

www.AlanaMcCarthy.com

CPSIA information can be obtained
at www.ICGtesting.com
Printed in the USA
BVHW021721080621
609010BV00004B/614